Blackbear the Pirate

Free Bring this book to LIFE with your PHONE or TABLET!

Blackbear the Pirate

Written by
Steve Buckley

Illustrated by
Ruth Palmer

More Blackbear the Pirate Adventures:

The Search for Captain Ben
Calico's Ghost
The Treasure Hunt

Published by Premiere
307 Orchard City Drive
Suite 210
Campbell, CA 95008 USA
info@fastpencil.com
http://premiere.fastpencil.com

3dMagicAction is a trademark of Courier Corporation

Manufactured in China by Oceanic Graphic International Inc.
33402101 2014

First Edition

For Katie, Brad, Stephanie & Danielle

**So that you may never grow up,
& I may never grow old.**

"Ahoy there maties!" said Blackbear the Pirate.

"Ahoy Captain Blackbear!" replied the crew.

"Prepare to set sail!" commanded Blackbear.

"Aye Aye, Captain," said Izzy Paws, the first mate,
"Where we be a heading?"

"We head South," responded Blackbear.

"To the island of Bearataria."

"Hold on there Capt'n, do ye mean to say, Bearataria?" inquired Calico, the saltiest seabear in Blackbear's crew.

"BEARATARIA" squawked Pawly the Parrot, as he sat upon Calico's shoulder.

"Not Bearataria!" exclaimed Bonnie, one of the two girls that sailed the seas with Blackbear.

"I'm not sure I like this idea," grumbled Barty, the oldest and wisest member of the crew.

"I smell adventure a brewing," whispered Izzy to Blackbear.

"Weigh anchor and get us under way, Mr. Paws!" ordered Blackbear the Pirate.

The anchor was raised as Blackbear and his faithful crew set sail aboard the Annie, Blackbear's grand pirate ship.

"Why are we going to Bearataria?" asked LeKidd, the youngest member of the crew.

"We go in search of the cave of the great Pirate King, Bearfoot," explained Blackbear.

"Aye there Capt'n, do ye mean to say we seek the cave of Bearfoot?" questioned Calico.

"BEARFOOT!" squawked Pawly the Parrot.

"What if I do not wish to meet the Pirate King, Bearfoot?" asked Bonnie.

"I don't think this is a very good idea," muttered Barty.

"I smell a quarrel a brewing," whispered Izzy to Blackbear.

"We seek a great adventure," said Blackbear, "So we go to Bearataria to find the cave of the great Pirate King, Bearfoot."

As they sailed across the deep blue sea the clouds
grew dark and the waves grew rough as wind and
rain tossed the Annie about upon the sea.

"Aye there Capt'n, me thinks we should bring the Annie about, and go back!" shouted Calico.

"GO BACK!" squawked Pawly the Parrot.

"The Sea is getting too rough!" exclaimed Bonnie.

"I think I'm going to be sick!" moaned LeKidd.

"I knew that this was not a good idea," griped Barty.

"I smell a storm a brewing," whispered Izzy to Blackbear.

"Batten down the hatches and secure the deck!" ordered Blackbear.

Blackbear the Pirate was a very good captain, and he guided the Annie through the raging wind and rain until the storm had passed.

"Aye there Capt'n, are ye sure ye don't need some sort of map so's we don't get lost?" demanded Calico.

"GET LOST!" squawked Pawly the Parrot.

"How much longer until we see land?" inquired Bonnie.

"Are we lost?" asked LeKidd.

"How about if we come up with a new idea," suggested Barty.

"I smell a mutiny a brewing," whispered Izzy to Blackbear.

"Belay that talk!" commanded Blackbear, "In the morning we arrive at Bearataria."

Blackbear the Pirate was a very good sailor, and he sailed the
Annie all through the night.

Early the next morning LeKidd spied an island.

"Land ho!" yelled LeKidd from the crow's nest, "I see an island!"

"Aye there Capt'n, tis Bearataria to be sure, and there be no scarier place" said Calico.

"NO SCARIER PLACE!" squawked Pawly the Parrot.

"I don't care for the looks of that island!" asserted Bonnie, "I think I'll stay with the Annie."

"I said from the beginning that this was not a good idea," insisted Barty.

"I smell fear a brewing," whispered Izzy to Blackbear.

"Drop the anchor and lower the longboat!" ordered Blackbear the Pirate.

Blackbear the Pirate was not afraid,
and he sent the crew into
the long boat. They rowed to the island, and once on shore
they saw a great challenge lay before them.

"Is Bearfoot's cave up there?" stammered LeKidd as he pointed to the top of a giant rock.

"Aye there Capt'n, do ye mean for us to climb up that there Bearface Rock?" asked Calico.

"BEARFACE ROCK!" squawked Pawly the Parrot.

"We have to climb up that huge rock?" cried Bonnie.

"This is turning out to be a really bad idea!" announced Barty.

"I smell a scrap a brewing," whispered Izzy to Blackbear.

"Come along," commanded Blackbear, "The cave of Bearfoot sits high atop Bearface Rock, and I'll show you the way."

Blackbear the Pirate was a great leader, and he led his crew as they began to climb to the top of Bearface Rock.

"This looks awfully steep to me!" whined LeKidd.

"Aye there Capt'n, me thinks it be about time we be heading back to the Annie," suggested Calico.

"BACK TO THE ANNIE!" squawked Pawly the Parrot.

"I'm afraid I'm going to fall," worried Bonnie.

"This is just one bad idea after another!" complained Barty.

"I smell trouble a brewing," whispered Izzy to Blackbear.

"Look!" shouted Blackbear, "We have made it to the top of Bearface Rock."

Blackbear the Pirate was a bold pirate, and after taking his crew to the top of Bearface Rock they came before a dark and menacing cave.

"Arrrhhhg!" came a booming voice from inside the cave,
"Who goes there?"

"What wa-wa-was that?" stuttered LeKidd.

"Aye there Capt'n, are ye believing we need to be a going into that cave?" asked Calico.

"INTO THAT CAVE!" squawked Pawly the Parrot.

"I'm not taking one step closer to that cave!" assured Bonnie.

"Going into that cave would be the worst idea ever!" declared Barty.

"I smell danger a brewing," whispered Izzy to Blackbear.

"It is I, Blackbear the Pirate, and my crew," proclaimed Blackbear, "We sailed here aboard my ship, the Annie."

"Why?" demanded the voice, "Why did you cross the stormy seas to come to Bearataria, and why did you face the danger of climbing Bearface Rock to stand before the cave of the great Pirate King, Bearfoot?"

Blackbear the Pirate was a clever pirate, and he knew it was time to show his crew that he was true to his words.

"Why?" replied Blackbear as he looked upon his crew, "We came in search of great adventure, of course, and I believe we found it."

With that, the crew all smiled and said "Aye Captain, we did, this was indeed a great adventure."

With their quest behind them, Blackbear the Pirate and his faithful crew went back to the Annie to set sail in search of their next GREAT ADVENTURE.

"Hey, where did everybody go?" wondered Bearfoot.